DAISY and DOODLE

DAISY and DOODLE

Story and pictures by **URSULA LANDSHOFF**

Bradbury Press Inc., Englewood Cliffs, N.J.

for Plush

The text of this book is set in 18 pt. Univers No. 55. The pictures are three-color pre-separated ink and wash drawings, reproduced in line and halftone.

Here is Daisy. She has no brothers or sisters.

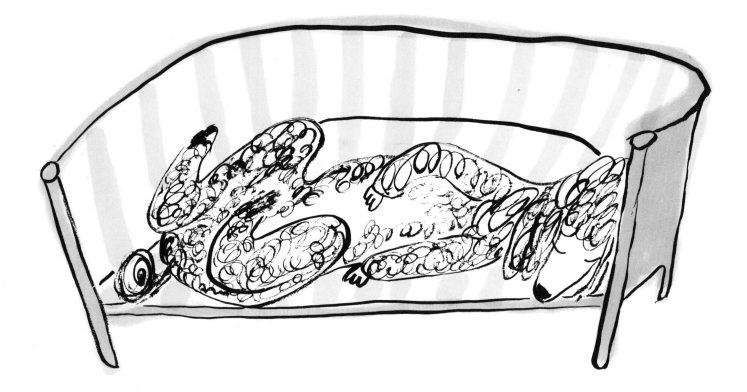

But she has a dog called Doodle. He sleeps by her bed,

sits by her chair

and walks by her feet.

Doodle watches Daisy. Daisy watches him.

They live with Daisy's mother and father in a big, crowded city.

One day they all went to the beach to run in the sun
and try out the water.

Even the beach was crowded. A lifeguard was watching everybody from high above.

But Doodle and Daisy found an empty beach where Doodle could run and chase the birds.

Beach dogs arrived from all sides. Doodle was busy
making friends.

When Daisy whistled, Doodle did not come.

Daisy took off her shoes and went into the water alone.

The ocean was cool and smooth and big.

Doodle saw Daisy. He wanted to go to her.

She looked very happy.

But then a wave knocked Daisy over. Doodle couldn't see
her any more.

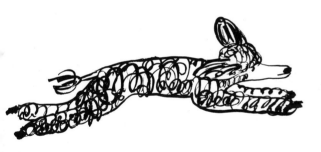

He ran for help.

The other dogs barked and barked.

The lifeguard ran to his boat, with Doodle close behind him.

People on the beach came running.

The dogs barked. The people waited silently.

And then they saw the lifeguard's boat on top of a wave.

In it sat Daisy, small but proud. Doodle was watching his Daisy again.

Back on the beach, Daisy's father lifted her up high and carried her around, smiling.

The ice cream man gave treats to dogs and people.

"Thank you," said Daisy to the lifeguard. And thank you, thought Doodle, thank you for saving my Daisy.

Daisy and Doodle rode home together happily.